Fairy Tales from Wales

Myrddin ap Dafydd
Translated by Siân Lewis
Illustrated by Graham Howells

First published: May 2005

© text: Myrddin ap Dafydd 2005
© illustrations: Graham Howells 2005
© English text: Siân Lewis 2005

ISBN: 0-86381-982-6

Cover design: Design Department of the Welsh Books Council

Published with the financial support of the
Welsh Books Council

Printed in Italy

Published by
Gwasg Carreg Gwalch, 12 Iard yr Orsaf, Llanrwst, Wales LL26 0EH
℡ 01492 642031 📠 01492 641502
📧 books@carreg-gwalch.co.uk
Internet: www.carreg-gwalch.co.uk

Contents

Who were the Fairies?

These stories are about the little people – the fairies – who have been part of Welsh life for hundreds of years. Though people had great respect for fairies in the old days, they were rather scared of them too!

The fairies were about the same size as small children. They often wore green clothes and they loved music and dancing. They had their own country, which could be reached through a cave, or the bottom of a lake or through a river bed. The fairies were very rich and they owned remarkable animals. Their time was not the same as our time. There are many stories of people who thought they had spent a night dancing with the fairies, but who discovered, to their great dismay the next day, that they had been away for many years.

The fairies had magic gifts and powers and were full of tricks. Yet they were also very kind to the poor and to those who helped them – but if you betrayed their secret, look out!

Fairy Gold

The fairies' greatest delight was merry music and dancing. They could dance all night!

This is the story of how Shenkin the fiddler got involved with the fairies. One night, when he was walking home across a lonely heath, he noticed a row of lights twinkling in the darkness nearby. He went to investigate and came upon a fine palace. He was quite sure that the palace had not been there when he had passed earlier in the day. Feeling rather nervous he moved closer, and a crowd of little people danced through the palace doorway and called to him:

"Shenkin! Shenkin! Come and play your fiddle for us!"

Shenkin was delighted with the invitation, because he knew that only the best musicians were chosen to play for the fairies. He took the fiddle from the satchel on his back and followed the little people into the palace.

Shenkin played dance tunes on his fiddle in the magnificent hall. The fairies whirled around in a bright, happy crowd, weaving in and out as lightly as air. Then Shenkin played livelier, wilder tunes. He felt as if he'd never played so well in his life. Watching the fairies dance so nimbly had given him a strange energy.

Tune after tune, dance after dance – no one was counting and no one cared how late it was. At last one of the little people called to him:

"Shenkin! That's enough for now! Come and have something to eat. You must be exhausted."

They took Shenkin to a table that was laden with delicious food. After he'd eaten, the poor fiddler could hardly keep his eyes open. He felt so tired, he could have slept on a pincushion! He saw a green chair that was long, soft and comfortable, and he sat down for a short rest. Soon he was stretched out on the chair and snoring loudly.

When Shenkin woke up, the fairies . . . the palace . . . the soft green chair – they had all disappeared. He was lying on a grassy mound with his fiddle and satchel beside him.

He got up and rubbed his eyes. As he did so, he heard a clinking sound in his pocket. What could it be? Shenkin was a poor fiddler who never had much money. He slid his hand into his pocket and to his surprise found a little bag containing twenty gold coins. A fortune! It was his payment for playing the fiddle at the fairy dance.

He set off home with a smile on his face. He imagined how pleased his wife would be! Just in time he came to his senses. He must tell no one about the fairy gold. If he did, the fairies would take back their treasure. So when he arrived home, Shenkin climbed up to the attic of his little cottage and hid the bag of gold in the thatched roof.

Some time later Shenkin's wife was fretting and sighing because they were so poor. Shenkin felt sorry for her. He sneaked up into the attic and on his return to the kitchen he pressed a gold piece into her hand without saying a word.

"Where did you get this gold?" she asked in amazement. "Have you any more? Are we rich?"

For days Shenkin's wife pestered him with questions. In the end he whispered his secret to her.

"Twenty gold pieces!" shrieked his wife. "Let me see the treasure!"

When Shenkin pulled the little sack from the thatched roof, there was no clink of coins. He opened it and – to the great dismay of his wife and himself – found that there was nothing inside but a handful of cockleshells. That was his punishment for betraying the fairies' secret.

A Castle of Sand

If you go to the Gower peninsula today, you may come across Pennard castle – a fine castle that stands facing the sea with its feet sunk deep in the yellow sand of the bay. Some say that this castle is under a spell cast by the fairies.

Many years ago, the Normans came to this country and tried to steal the land from the Welsh. When the Welsh refused to surrender to them, the Normans built many castles to show how rich and powerful they were. One proud Norman came to the Gower and built Pennard castle.

This Norman was a cruel and selfish man. When he wasn't hunting the Welsh, he enjoyed hunting the animals that lived in the wooded valley behind the castle. One day, he came across a pretty little Welsh girl dancing merrily in front of her friends in a clearing in the woods. He stopped to watch and admire her.

"We could do with some entertainment in that cold grey castle of ours," said the Norman to his men. "Grab that girl and take her back to the castle!"

The girl was captured and locked in a room in the castle tower. There she wept and wept. Her heart was breaking. But no one in the castle understood her language and no one bothered to listen. The Norman had a heart as stony as the walls of his castle. He went back to his hunting.

The fairies love all those who enjoy music and dancing. In the woods little eyes had seen the soldiers kidnapping the girl. On the beach little ears had heard her sad weeping.

That night the Norman came home starving after a good day's hunting. He called for food and drink. He and his soldiers and servants were enjoying a banquet in the great hall when suddenly a mighty wind rose in the bay outside. The wind scooped sand from the beach and hurled it at the castle. In the hall one or two of the men noticed the sand blowing under the door and through the arrow slits in the walls.

Soon the flagstones were covered in a thin carpet of sand. When the sand had risen to cover the soldiers' shoes, one or two began to feel uneasy.

Soon the sand had reached their knees. A couple of soldiers struggled through the thick layer of sand and ran for their lives from the castle.

Before long a sandstorm was whirling through the castle. Some of the Normans were already trapped in their seats and could not escape. It was so hard to breathe that the Norman lord had to wrap his cloak round his face. Gradually the sand filled his mouth and his lungs.

The wild storm raged all night. The Normans now knew it was no ordinary storm. It was a magic storm − a storm whipped up by the fairies to take revenge on the proud Norman for imprisoning the little dancer.

And what happened to the little dancer? The wind blew the sand into a great heap against the castle tower until it reached the window of her room. She stepped out of the window, slid down the sand drift and returned home safely to her family in the woods.

By morning there was not a single Norman left in the area, and Pennard castle had disappeared beneath the dunes. Only the tips of its turrets could be seen poking up from the sand.

Through the years people tried many times to clear the sand from Pennard castle. But no matter how much sand was removed by day, the sea winds would blow it all back during the night.

No one has managed to live there since then. Some say that the castle is still bewitched. But the little dancer's descendants have remained in the area and the family still tell the story of how she was saved long ago by a fairy storm.

The Stray Cow

The Welsh Black cow is famous throughout the
world. It is a strong and hardy little cow, a good
breeder that can survive hard winters without
difficulty. The Welsh Black is part of our landscape.
But few realise that it is a fairy cow. Above Aberdyfi
in the mountains of Meirionnydd lies a lake called
the Bearded Lake – it's called the Bearded Lake
because reeds and rushes grow thickly in the water
and look like a covering of hair. At the bottom of
the lake they say there used to be a gateway to
Fairyland. The little people were often seen with
their white dogs and milk-white cows along the
shores of the lake. No one could get near these
strange animals, and every evening they were all
led into the lake by the fairies and disappeared.

At Drws y Nant, a stone's throw from the
lake, lived a poor farmer. All he owned were two
scrawny old cows. Every night he would look
longingly at the fairy cattle as they disappeared
into the lake.

"I wouldn't mind having one of those fine
fairy cows," said the farmer out loud.

One morning, when the farmer went out to milk his two cows, he found one of the fairy cattle in the field with them. The sleek white cow gave the farmer a very settled, contented look, as if to say she'd made up her mind to stay with her new friends.

At first the farmer was worried that the little people might think he had stolen one of their cows. But no harm came to him and he soon realised that the cow was a gift. Her milk was delicious and made excellent butter and cheese. Drws y Nant dairy produce soon made a name for itself in the market place, and the farmer was able to ask a good price for it. Within a few months the white cow had given birth to two calves that were good quality animals like their mother. Within a few years the farmer was very rich indeed!

But he became too greedy. He noticed that the first cow had grown rather fat, so he decided to slaughter her for meat.

The butcher arrived one day, followed by a big crowd who had come to witness the slaughter of the famous cow. When the butcher raised his arm to plunge his knife into the cow, the crowd heard an unearthly scream. The butcher's arm was paralysed and his sharp knife fell to the ground.

Over by the lake the farmer saw a slender woman dressed in green. She called the cows home with a strange song: "Come, stray white cow, come home to me now. With your calves one and all, come home when I call."

In that high valley the ground shook as dozens of white cows stampeded towards the bearded waters of the lake. The farmer ran after them, but by the time he had reached the shore the slender woman and the cows were sinking quickly towards the bottom of the lake. The woman turned round and waved at him scornfully before disappearing.

The cows too gave a mocking wave of their tails – and in a moment there was nothing left but a few ripples on the surface of the water.

There was one small consolation for the farmer. One of the cows had chosen to stay behind. By the time he returned home, she had lost her milk-white coat and had turned black. She was a young cow, who had not yet grown to her full height – and from that day she never grew any bigger.

She lived to a ripe old age and, although she was rather small, she was very productive. From this fairy cow came the breed of Welsh Black cattle that are now so much at home on the hills and mountains of Wales.

The Land of the Fair Folk

Einion was a shepherd in the Preseli mountains in Pembrokeshire and he knew that area like the back of his hand. But one day he got lost in a thick fog and found himself inside a ring of dark green grass. He was very much afraid, because he knew he had walked into a fairy ring.

Try as he might, Einion could not escape from the ring. He was dripping with sweat and shaking with fear, when a mild-mannered old man with blue eyes came up to him.

"I'm trying to find my way home," said Einion.

"I know that. Follow me," said the old man.

They came to a large round stone and the old man struck it three times with his stick. The stone moved aside to reveal a narrow entrance and steps that led down into the depths of the earth.

"Follow me," said the old man again. "Don't be afraid. No harm will come to you."

Soon they reached a rich beautiful, wooded land with fine palaces and sparkling rivers. The birds sang sweetly and the earth itself seemed to smile. Einion knew then he was in Fairyland, the land of the Fair Folk.

They came to the old man's palace. The shepherd was astonished and delighted to see the musical instruments, the gold and silver plates and the dishes of food that came to the table of their own accord! He heard voices speaking in a strange language, though there was no one to be seen.

He tried to speak to the old man, but found he could neither move his tongue nor say a word. A beautiful lady came to them and three of the fairest young women in the world. The young women smiled at him slyly. Again Einion tried to speak and again he failed.

Then one of the young women came up to him, ran her fingers through his wavy hair and planted a kiss on his lips. At once Einion's tongue was loosened. Not only could he speak again, but he could also understand the fairies' language.

For a whole year he remained there, bewitched by the land itself and by that girl's red mouth.

As time went by, Einion began to miss his old home. He asked the old man, who was the king of the fairies, if he could go back for a while to the land of his mother and father. Olwen, the girl who had kissed him, was disappointed.

"You will never come back to see me," she said.

Her words sent a chill through Einion, but once he had promised to return, he was allowed to go. The fairies gave him fine clothes and plenty of gold for the journey.

When he reached his old home, he found that everything had changed. No one recognised him, because our time passes much faster than fairy time. Some of the old people remembered the story about a shepherd who had got lost on the mountain long ago.

Einion told no one where he had been. Everyone was amazed at his fine clothes and many asked him how he had become so rich.

But in time Einion began to miss Fairyland and all the friends he had made there. So one day he decided to leave his old home once more.

When Einion returned to Fairyland, everyone was pleased to see him. Olwen gave him a warm welcome. Soon they were married and living happily together.

After a while Einion longed to visit his old home again, and this time he wanted to take his wife with him. He begged the fairy king to let them go, and at long last he agreed. He gave them rich gifts and two snow-white ponies for the journey.

Everyone in the old country was delighted with Olwen. They thought there was no one as beautiful as her in the whole world. When their son, Taliesin, was born, he too was a fine, handsome lad.

All the old women of the area did their best to find out who Olwen was and where she had come from.

"Is she one of the Fair Folk?" one of them asked Einion.

"She is indeed fair," the shepherd replied with a smile. "And if you could see her two sisters, you'd know that all her folk are fair too!"

Fair play to Einion, he managed to keep the fairies' secret to the end!

Tales from Wales 2
King Arthur's Cave

Imagine the surprise of a young shepherd who discovers a cave full of treasure and sleeping soldiers . . .

Tales from Wales 3
The Faithful Dog, Gelert

The haunting story of Prince Llywelyn's favourite dog, the baby in the cradle and the wolf . . .

Tales from Wales 4
Black Bart, the Welsh Pirate

Did you know that the most successful and colourful pirate ever was a Welshman . . . ?